It's Fall!

By Linda Glaser

Illustrated by Susan Swan

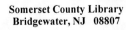
M Millbrook Press

Minneapolis

To my dear friend Robin, a fellow nature lover. We share more
than 25 years of memories enjoying the outdoors together.

Special thanks to Billie Anderson and Ruth Worley, both
kindergarten teachers extraordinaire, for their expertise and enthusiasm.
LG

For my stellar brother, Richard Swan, his wonderful
wife, Shirley, and their magical daughter, Catherine.
SS

Text copyright © 2001 by Linda Glaser
Illustrations © 2001 by Susan Swan

Millbrook Press, Inc.
A division of Lerner Publishing Group
241 First Avenue North
Minneapolis, MN 55401 USA

Website address: www.lernerbooks.com

Library of Congress Cataloging-in-Publication Data
Glaser, Linda.
It's fall! / by Linda Glaser ; illustrated by Susan Swan.
p. cm. — (I love the seasons!)
Summary: A child experiences the colors and textures of fall.
ISBN-13: 978–0–7613–1758–6 (lib. bdg. : alk. paper)
ISBN-10: 0–7613–1758–9 (lib. bdg. : alk. paper)
ISBN-13: 978–0–7613–1342–7 (pbk. : alk. paper)
ISBN-10: 0–7613–1342–7 (pbk. : alk. paper)

[1. Autumn—Fiction.] I. Swan, Susan, ill. II. Title. III. Series.
PZ7.G48047 It 2001   [E]—dc21   00-048168

Manufactured in the United States of America
8 9 10 11 12 13 – DP – 11 10 09 08 07 06

It's Fall!

I skip and swish through autumn leaves.
They crunch and crackle under my feet
and whoosh and whirl all around me.

Red, orange, yellow, gold, and brown.
A wind swoops up.
More leaves fall down.

It's fall! I help rake a big, big pile of leaves.
Whee! I jump in and sink deep, deep, deep.
I hide inside. It smells sharp and sweet.
Leaves prickle and tickle all over me.
I wait and wait. Then. . .

Pop! It's me!

We hear the wild honking of migrating geese
as they fly way up overhead in V's.
A hawk soars up in a sweeping glide.
And there go some monarch butterflies!

They're all heading south where it's warm,
because colder days are coming soon.

It's fall!
Animals are hiding all around me.
They're getting ready to hibernate in deep, deep sleep.
Ladybugs hide in pinecones and under bark and leaves.
Earthworms tunnel way down where the earth doesn't freeze.

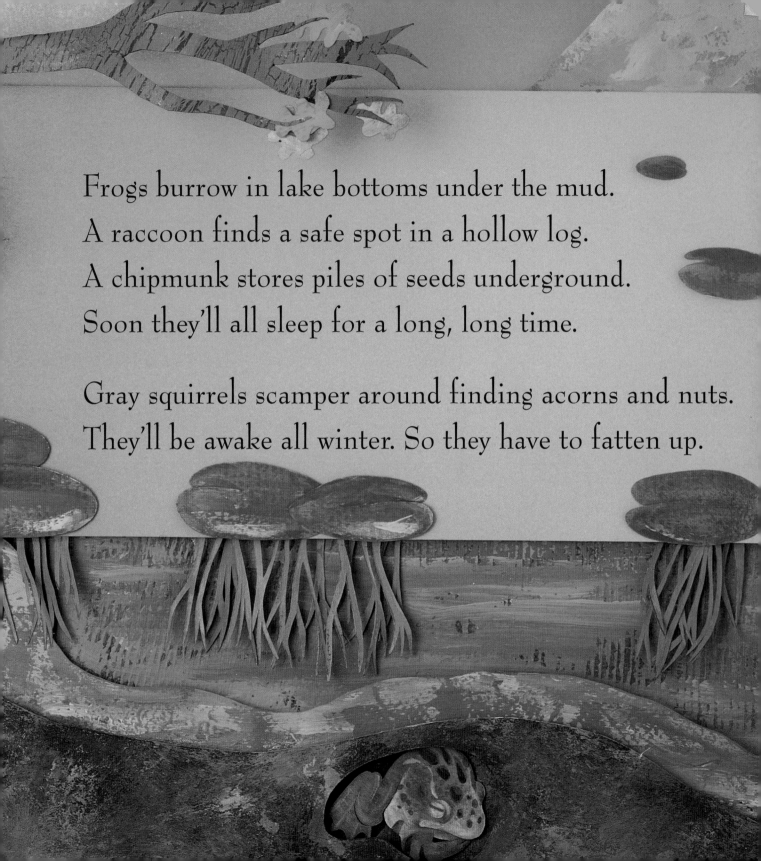

Frogs burrow in lake bottoms under the mud.
A raccoon finds a safe spot in a hollow log.
A chipmunk stores piles of seeds underground.
Soon they'll all sleep for a long, long time.

Gray squirrels scamper around finding acorns and nuts.
They'll be awake all winter. So they have to fatten up.

It's fall!
The air is turning crisp and cold.
It's time to wear our warmer clothes.
We put on jackets and pants and long sleeves
to keep us warm when it turns breezy.

The sun goes down so early now.
We wait and watch the sky grow dark.
We see the great big harvest moon
rise up and up and up.

Wherever we go we find flowers and weeds
drying out and scattering seeds.
We float silky parachutes of dry milkweed.
Birds land on our dry sunflowers and eat the seeds.

Tall, dry cattails whisper and rattle.
Crisp leaves swish and rustle and chatter.
It's fall!

We collect acorns and pinecones and pretty leaves.
I choose a great big pumpkin.
We carve a face and roast the seeds.

One day in our garden we dig some holes.
We plant crocuses and tulips and daffodil bulbs.
I try to picture how they'll look a long time from
now when they finally come up.

Then one day I notice that the trees are all bare.
Leaves have fallen everywhere.
There's an icy chill in the air.
Soon, very soon, winter will be here.
But right now, it's still fall.

I gather handfuls of autumn leaves.
I toss them up. They swirl down on me.
It's fall! It's fall!
I love it all! It's fall!

Nature Activities to Do in the Fall

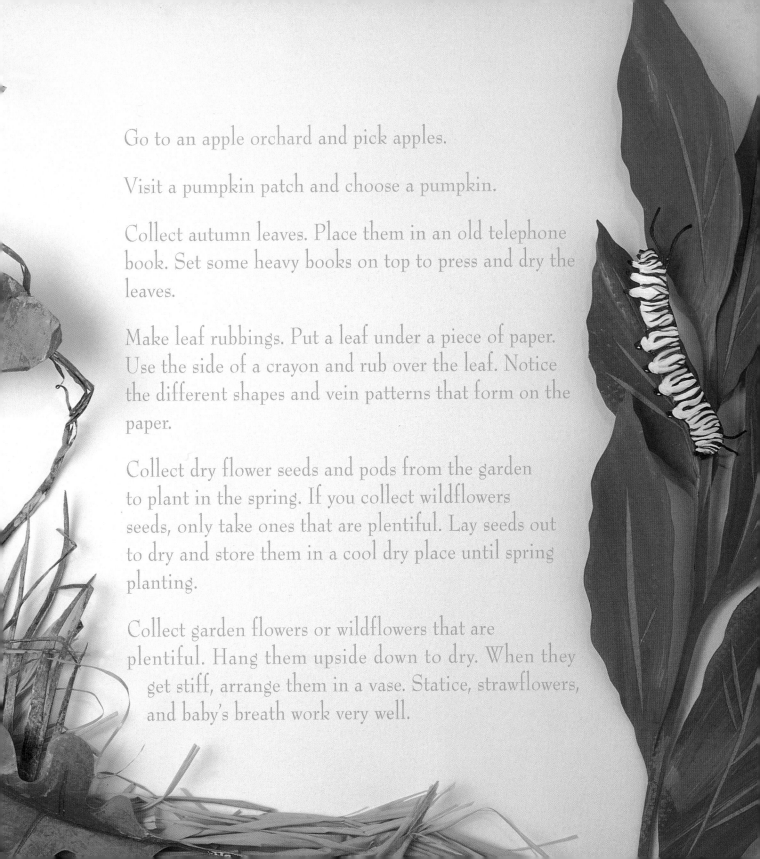

Go to an apple orchard and pick apples.

Visit a pumpkin patch and choose a pumpkin.

Collect autumn leaves. Place them in an old telephone book. Set some heavy books on top to press and dry the leaves.

Make leaf rubbings. Put a leaf under a piece of paper. Use the side of a crayon and rub over the leaf. Notice the different shapes and vein patterns that form on the paper.

Collect dry flower seeds and pods from the garden to plant in the spring. If you collect wildflowers seeds, only take ones that are plentiful. Lay seeds out to dry and store them in a cool dry place until spring planting.

Collect garden flowers or wildflowers that are plentiful. Hang them upside down to dry. When they get stiff, arrange them in a vase. Statice, strawflowers, and baby's breath work very well.

Compare seed pods that you find. Notice the many different ways that seeds travel.

Make a seed mosaic. Glue different seeds on stiff paper or cardboard in a pretty design or picture.

- In early fall find a field of milkweed with monarch eggs or monarch caterpillars. Collect a few. Also collect plenty of milkweed leaves to feed them. Watch the caterpillars grow and form chrysalides. Once they emerge, set the monarch butterflies free on a warm, sunny day.

If you plant milkweed seeds in your yard, milkweed plants will grow in the spring, and then monarch butterflies may come and lay eggs on them!

Plant your favorite flowering bulbs in the yard. After winter they will grow and bloom. If you don't have a yard, put the bulbs in the refrigerator for six weeks. Then plant them inside in a pot. Keep them watered and they will bloom in your house.

Plant
some large cloves of garlic
outside. They'll come up in the spring and be
ready for you to harvest late next summer.

Start a leaf compost pile. Pile leaves in a far corner of the yard. Let
the pile sit and decay. If you turn it over, it will decay faster. In a year or
two it will be all composted and ready to add to your garden.

Some fun things to plant in the summer for the fall harvest: gourds, pumpkins,
sunflowers. Some flowers that bloom in the fall if planted in spring: asters,
chrysanthemums, dahlias, black-eyed Susans, strawflowers, statice.

After dinner, go outside at night with a grown-up.
Watch the moon and stars appear.

Take photos of one tree all during fall and notice the changes.

Follow the migration of animals on Journey North on the Internet.
www.learner.org/jnorth

About the Author and Illustrator

Linda Glaser is the author of many successful nonfiction picture books on natural history subjects. Her books SPECTACULAR SPIDERS, COMPOST!, WONDERFUL WORMS, and OUR BIG HOME: AN EARTH POEM were all named Outstanding Science Trade Books for Children by the Children's Book Council/National Science Teachers Association. In addition to teaching and writing, she conducts writing workshops for schoolchildren and for adults. She lives in Minnesota.

For IT'S FALL, Susan Swan created three-dimensional cut-paper artwork. First she selected her papers and then hand painted them to get the colors and textures she needed to achieve the palette of fall. She then layered the papers to accomplish the dramatic sense of depth that gives life to each piece of art. Finally, Susan's husband, Terry, photographed the finished artwork with lighting that accents the shadows of the paper. Susan and her husband are, professionally, Swan & Rasberry Studios, and they live in Texas.